To my grandchildren,

Jakob and Nathan, Grandpop

and Grandma's "Best Boys".

A Day with Tuckey the Nantucket Whale

Copyright© 2015 by Robert Cameron

Requests for permission to make copies of any part of the work should be submitted online at rcameron@nantucket.net or mailed to Robert Cameron P.O. Box 975 Nantucket, MA 02554.

Library of Congress Control Number: 2015908529

PRBANG0615A

Printed in the United States

ISBN-13: 978-1-63177-260-3

www.mascotbooks.com

A Day With Tuckey

the Nantucket Whale

Written by
Robert Cameron

Illustrated by **Rod Cole**

It's a beautiful, sunny summer morning on Nantucket Sound. Blue skies are filled with large, puffy, white clouds. Can you see one in the shape of a whale? Oh wow!

A breeze fills the sails of the Rainbow Fleet moving gracefully on calm waters. Can you pick out each color of the rainbow? Red, blue, green, orange, yellow, and violet. What a beautiful sight!

Flying fish scoot along above the water.
Flying fish are really cool!

Merrily swimming deep underwater is Tuckey the Nantucket whale. He sure is a beauty! Tuckey comes to the surface and pops his head out to look around. He sees sailboats, fishing boats, flying fish, seagulls, and much more.

Fishing boats chug along with their lines and nets in the water. Soon they will head back to port to sell their fish. Many of us will enjoy fresh and delicious fish today. Yum!

Seagulls fly and squawk above the fishing boats. They wait to scoop up fish that fall out of the nets. Freddy has a fish! Do you see it hanging from his beak? Freddy is a local gull who searches the Nantucket waters every day for food. With a full tummy, he looks for somewhere to rest. Maybe a buoy, a small boat, or even a whale.

Tuckey sees his friend Freddy and calls to him. Freddy lands on top of Tuckey. A favorite spot for him to rest.

Freddy squawks, "I ate too many fish this morning and my tummy is full." Freddy flips the last fish from his beak into Tuckey's mouth.

Tuckey says, "Thanks for the nice surprise and tasty treat!"

After a lot of squawking, Freddy flies off as Tuckey dives into the water. He makes a big splash when his tail comes high out of the water. What good exercise!

Tuckey swims deep underwater. From time to time, he comes to the surface to puff mist from his blowhole on the top of his head and breathe air into his lungs. Blowholes are a whale's nostrils. A flap covers them when whales go below the surface so no water gets in the blowhole. Tuckey can only breathe through his blowhole, not his mouth.

Tuckey loves the clean, clear Nantucket waters. He can see all the way to the sandy ocean bottom. Everyone does their part to keep the waters clean so we can all enjoy them.

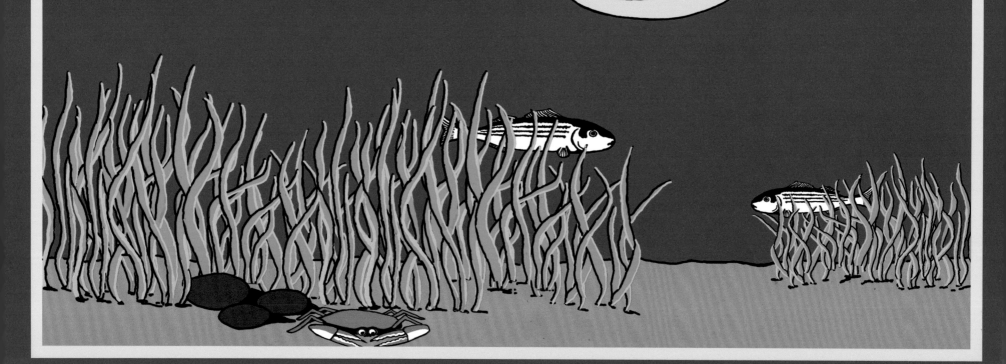

Another friend of Tuckey is Mr. Lobster. He has a reddish-brown body with two big claws. Tuckey looks forward to seeing him each day. He helps Mr. Lobster look for food on the ocean bottom.

Mr. Lobster says, "Crabs, clams, and mussels are my favorite!" It's always a lot of fun being with Mr. Lobster.

Tuckey knows it's going to be a fun and exciting day. He can't wait to get started. But first, he must eat his breakfast. We all know breakfast is a very important meal for everyone.

Tuckey lowers his head under the water, arches his spine, then lifts his tail out of the water. He dives deep underwater looking for food. His favorites are small fish and squid. He needs lots of them to fill his big tummy.

In the Nantucket waters, there are many fish. Can you see them? There are flounder, cod, halibut, and many others. Wow! Such a variety and treat for Tuckey.

After Tuckey's tummy is full, he swims to the surface to look around. Off at a distance, Tuckey sees a big boat. He swims over to get a better look.

Tuckey sees it's the Nantucket ferry. Seeing it brings a big smile to Tuckey's face. He enjoys the ferry because of the families with children and pets onboard. The ferry brings them to Nantucket Island.

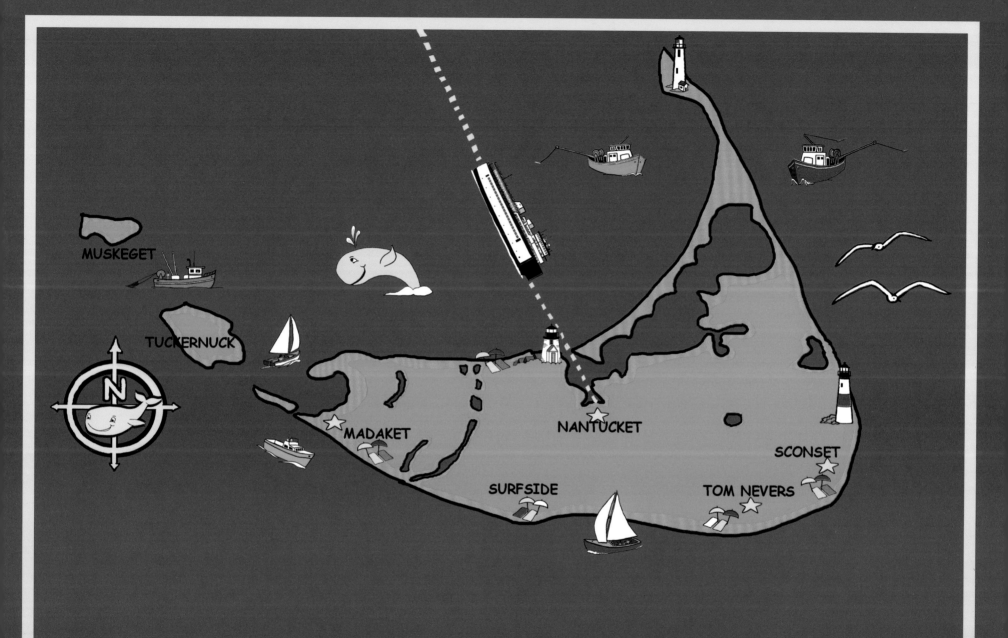

Nantucket Island is a very special place for families. There are so many fun and exciting things to do. They can go to the beach and build sandcastles, buy handmade ice cream cones, walk in town and cross cobblestone streets, bicycle on pathways out to Sconset, surf cast for small blues, and lots more. It's one of the best places for a family vacation.

Tuckey swims all around the ferry so he can see the families waving and the children's smiling faces. He even jumps out of the water and does some tricks. He's very acrobatic. He jumps high out of the water, turns on his side, and falls back down with a huge splash. Sometimes, it ends up being a belly flop! Tuckey loves to put on a show.

Families sit on the benches at the back of the ferry. They enjoy the nice weather and salty air. Dogs look over the handrail and bark happily at Tuckey.

The captain of the ferry stands on the bridge deck waving at Tuckey.

Tuckey swims extra fast to keep up with the ferry. The ferry's speed is about 15 miles per hour. Pretty fast!

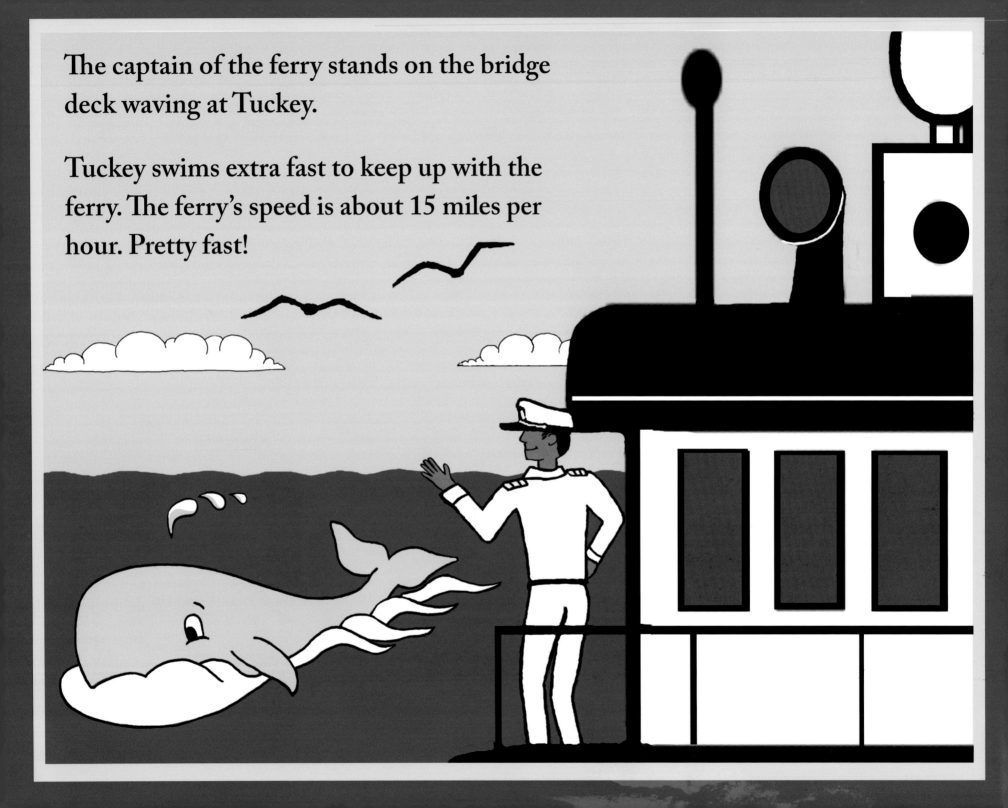

In the distance is Brant Point Lighthouse, the entrance to the Nantucket Harbor. Boats are entering the harbor, other boats are leaving. Some boats are tied to buoys. The harbor is a very busy place.

In the harbor, you must be extra careful to not collide with each other. To help prevent this, there are rules of the road for boats in the water. Everyone needs to be alert and proceed safely. Tuckey and the Nantucket ferry always obey these rules.

Doing things safely is a must. Tuckey learned this from his parents.

One of Tuckey's whale buddies got hurt while playing in the water. He wasn't paying attention and bumped into a small fishing boat. He got a bruise and wasn't able to play until it healed. He learned his lesson to obey the rules in the water.

Tuckey sees Freddy flying around. He comes over and plops down on Tuckey's head. Freddy is so glad to be with him. Tuckey says, "Look, Freddy. That's the dock where the Nantucket ferry is heading."

Tuckey hears the captain of the ferry announce, "We'll be docking at Nantucket Island in a few minutes." Families gather the things they are taking with them. Can you see their suitcases, bicycles, and fishing rods?

Tuckey and Freddy watch the ferry turn around and back towards the dock. The captain did a nice job steering the ferry alongside the dock. A job well done!

They watch the cars and trucks drive off the ferry. Fuel trucks deliver gasoline to the gas stations on the island. Other trucks deliver food and drinks to grocery stores. Cars drive down the ramp, taking families to all areas of the island.

Some families go down the outside steps of the ferry to meet friends and family waiting for them. Everyone is happy to see each other. They hug and kiss and can't wait to do all the fun things on Nantucket Island. Freddy squawks to Tuckey, "It impresses me each time seeing all this activity coming from one ferry. Truly amazing!"

The sun sets and the moon is out. Tuckey says to Freddy,
"You know what that means."

Freddy says, "Yes, it's time for families to get a good night's sleep."

"In the morning, all will be ready for another fun and adventurous day on
Nantucket Island."

Freddy squawks, "Yippee! Hooray to that!"

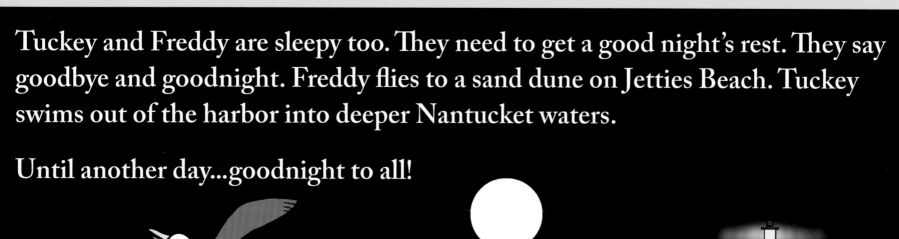

Tuckey and Freddy are sleepy too. They need to get a good night's rest. They say goodbye and goodnight. Freddy flies to a sand dune on Jetties Beach. Tuckey swims out of the harbor into deeper Nantucket waters.

Until another day...goodnight to all!

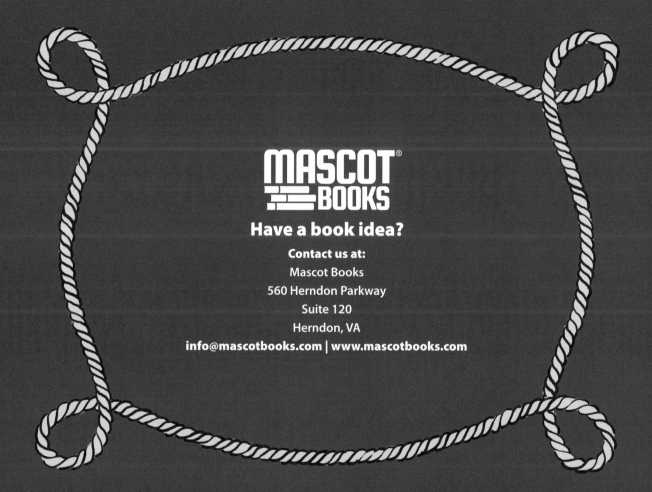